Dear Parents:

Congratulations! Your child is taking the first steps on an exciting journey. The destination? Independent reading!

STEP INTO READING® will help your child get there. The program offers five steps to reading success. Each step includes fun stories and colorful art or photographs. In addition to original fiction and books with favorite characters, there are Step into Reading Non-Fiction Readers, Phonics Readers and Boxed Sets, Sticker Readers, and Comic Readers—a complete literacy program with something to interest every child.

Learning to Read, Step by Step!

Ready to Read   Preschool–Kindergarten
• big type and easy words • rhyme and rhythm • picture clues
For children who know the alphabet and are eager to begin reading.

Reading with Help   Preschool–Grade 1
• basic vocabulary • short sentences • simple stories
For children who recognize familiar words and sound out new words with help.

Reading on Your Own   Grades 1–3
• engaging characters • easy-to-follow plots • popular topics
For children who are ready to read on their own.

Reading Paragraphs   Grades 2–3
• challenging vocabulary • short paragraphs • exciting stories
For newly independent readers who read simple sentences with confidence.

Ready for Chapters   Grades 2–4
• chapters • longer paragraphs • full-color art
For children who want to take the plunge into chapter books but still like colorful pictures.

STEP INTO READING® is designed to give every child a successful reading experience. The grade levels are only guides; children will progress through the steps at their own speed, developing confidence in their reading. The F&P Text Level on the back cover serves as another tool to help you choose the right book for your child.

Remember, a lifetime love of reading starts with a single step!

To Lee, Elinor, and Charlie . . . my 1, 2, 3
(in no particular order)

Copyright © 2014 by Tad Hills

All rights reserved. Published in the United States by Random House Children's Books,
a division of Random House LLC, a Penguin Random House Company, New York.

Step into Reading, Random House, and the Random House colophon are registered trademarks
of Random House LLC.

Visit us on the Web!
StepIntoReading.com
randomhousekids.com
Educators and librarians, for a variety of teaching tools, visit us at RHTeachersLibrarians.com

Library of Congress Cataloging-in-Publication Data
Hills, Tad, author, illustrator.
Rocket's 100th day of school / Tad Hills. — First edition.
pages cm
Summary: Rocket the dog is excited about the 100th day of school and enlists the help of his
friends to collect one hundred special things to bring to class, from heart-shaped stones found
with Mr. Barker to feathers Owl provides, but will he find enough items in time?
ISBN 978-0-385-39095-8 (hc) — ISBN 978-0-385-39096-5 (glb) — ISBN 978-0-385-39097-2 (pbk.)
ISBN 978-0-385-39098-9 (ebk)
[1. Collectors and collecting—Fiction. 2. Hundredth day of school—Fiction. 3. Schools—Fiction.
4. Friendship—Fiction. 5. Dogs—Fiction.] I. Title. II. Title: Rocket's one hundredth day of school.
PZ7.H563737Rof 2014
[E]—dc23
2014010940

The illustrations in this book were rendered in colored pencils and acrylic paint.

Printed in the United States of America
10 9 8 7 6 5 4 3 2 1

This book has been officially leveled by using the F&P Text Level Gradient™ Leveling System.

Rocket's
100th
Day
of
School

Tad Hills

Random House 🏠 New York

Rocket needs to find
100 special things
for the 100th day
of school.

He finds

the perfect spot to keep

his special things.

Or maybe not.

"You can keep your
things here," says Bella.

Rocket finds pencils.

He finds a book.

He finds acorns.

He puts them
in the tree.

Emma helps Rocket
find red leaves
and pinecones.

Mr. Barker helps Rocket
find heart-shaped stones.

Fred helps Rocket
find sticks that look
like numbers.

Rocket writes down
all 26 letters
of the alphabet.

He puts everything
in the tree.

Some days
he writes down words
he likes.

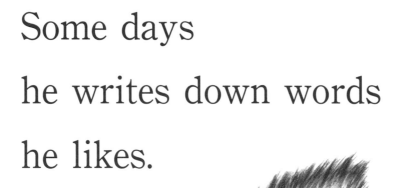

Owl gives
Rocket feathers.

They all go
in the tree.

Finally,
the 100th day of school
is here.

Rocket runs to the tree.

He counts everything
he put in there.

10 pencils
1 book
18 red leaves
5 pinecones
3 stones
5 sticks
26 letters
23 words
+4 feathers
_____
95 things

"Where are the acorns?"
Rocket asks.

"Have you seen the
acorns, Bella?"

"The what?"
Bella asks.

"The acorns," says Rocket.

"Acorns?" asks Bella.

"Yes," says Rocket.

"YES!
    I ATE THEM!"
shouts Bella.

"I LOVE ACORNS
    SO MUCH!"

"I need those acorns!"
says Rocket.

"It is the 100th day
of school.
Now I only have
95 things!"

cils
k
leaves
econes
nes
icks
tters
rds
thers
hings

Rocket has an idea.

"Follow me, everyone,"
says Rocket.

"We are <u>all</u>

going to school."

"95 plus four <u>old</u>
friends makes 99,"
counts Rocket.

"And one <u>new</u> friend
makes 100!"